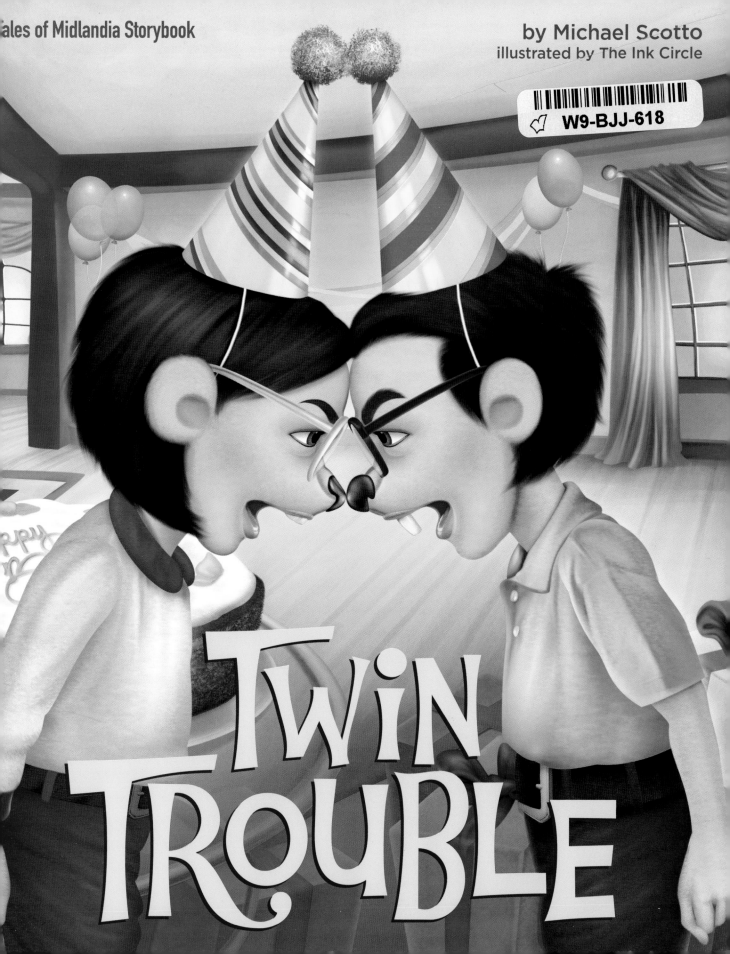

Tales of Midlandia Storybook

by Michael Scotto
illustrated by The Ink Circle

Twin Trouble

WELCOME TO MIDLANDIA

OUR STORY BEGINS

Midlandia University

Community Center

Playland Park

Animal Land

HERE

Town Square

Bike Factory

Harvest Farms

TWIN TROUBLE

by Michael Scotto

illustrated by The Ink Circle

Brushy and Fixit were brother and sister. But they were a unique kind of brother and sister: **They were twins!**

These siblings were alike in many ways.

"We have the exact same smile, sis!" Brushy said.

"We are both the same height," Fixit noted. **"Isn't that cool?"**

But like many brothers and sisters, Brushy and Fixit argued a lot. When they were younger, it seemed like they did nothing but fight.

At home: "Your hair can wait," Brushy said. "I still need to floss!"
"It'll be next week before you're done!" Fixit complained.

At the playground: "Watch it!" Fixit cried. "You almost broke my glasses!"

"Then you should keep your glasses out of my way," Brushy replied.

Even at the theater: "Oww, stop poking my ribs!" Brushy hissed.

"I'm not poking your ribs, silly," Fixit whispered. "I'm poking your sternum!"

Just like every brother and sister, Brushy and Fixit had their ups and their downs. But no one in Midlandia had been prepared for their biggest fight.

It had happened at the twins' birthday party. They had just reached the age where Midlandians began to decide what to do as grown-ups.

As Chief Tatupu served the carrot cake, Brushy took Fixit aside. "I have exciting news!" Brushy told her. "I have decided what I want to do for a job."

"What a coincidence," Fixit said. "I've decided too! We should make an announcement."

"Great idea, sis!" Brushy said. "You can go first."

"Thanks!" Fixit said. **"You're the best brother ever."**

Ding-ding-ding! Fixit clinked a fork against her glass of birthday punch. "When Midlandians grow up, we each get to choose what job we want," she said. "I've made my choice. **I want to be a doctor!**"

Everyone in the crowd clapped...but Brushy only scowled.

"No!" Brushy said.
"You can't be a doctor!"
Fixit was stunned. "Why not?" she asked.

"Because...I want to be a doctor!" Brushy replied.

"We can't both be doctors," Fixit shouted. "Stop copying me!"

"I've never copied in my life!" Brushy snorted.

Knowing how Brushy and Fixit sometimes fought, Chief Tatupu tried to calm things down. "It is your birthday, you two," he said. "There is no need to fight."

The twins paid Chief no mind.

"I said I wanted to be a doctor first," Fixit argued.

"Only because I let you speak first!" Brushy cried. "You've made a real mess of things now."

"You want a mess?" Fixit asked. She dug her hand into their birthday cake and rubbed a piece right in Brushy's face! **"That's a mess."**

Brushy wiped the cake from his eyes.
"Two can play at this game," he declared.
The twins chased each other around the room, throwing cake and anything else they could get their hands on.

"Oh!" Fixit screamed. **"You're the worst brother ever!"**

I have to stop this before someone gets hurt!
Chief thought. As Chief ran toward the fighting twins,
Brushy lifted the punch bowl over his head.

"How about a bath?" Brushy said, and he
dumped the whole bowl onto Fixit.

"Ack, you punched me!" Fixit cried.

Brushy tossed the empty bowl behind him...and it
bonked Chief right on the head!

"Ouch!" he yelped. **"My noggin!"**

"Look what you did now, you big meanie!" Fixit yelled at her brother.

"That is enough!" Chief said, and he grabbed each twin by the collar to hold them apart. "**This party is over, everyone.**"

While Brushy mopped up the food fight, Fixit got Chief some ice and a bandage for the bump on his head.

"You need to stop this fighting,"
Chief told the twins.
"I try to get along with Fixit," Brushy
huffed, "but sometimes, I get so mad at her!"
"I get mad at Brushy, too," Fixit said.

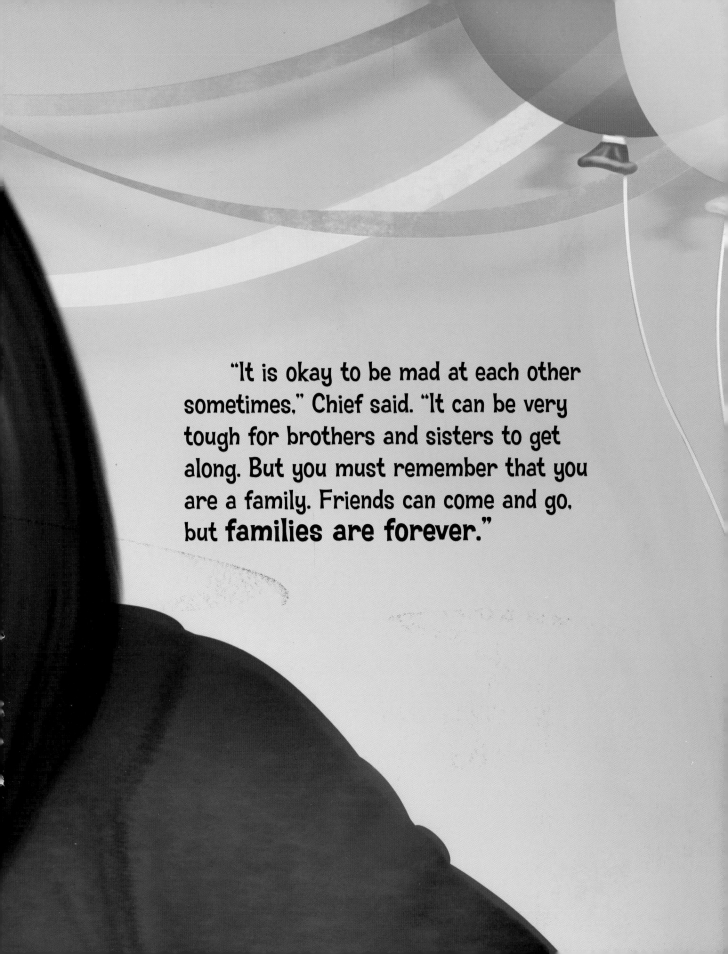

"It is okay to be mad at each other sometimes," Chief said. "It can be very tough for brothers and sisters to get along. But you must remember that you are a family. Friends can come and go, but **families are forever.**"

"I'm sorry for starting a fight with you," Brushy told Fixit.

"I'm sorry for saying you were a bad brother," Fixit told Brushy.

"This is more like it," Chief said. "It is always better to calmly share your feelings rather than yell or fight. Now, let us try to solve this doctor problem."

After a long talk, the twins found an answer. Perhaps they could both become doctors after all! At the University of Midlandia, Fixit and Brushy studied what interested each of them most. Fixit learned about bones, bumps, and bruises, while Brushy focused on teeth and tartar.

Once the twins finished school, Fixit became known as Doc Fixit. She used her skills to bandage, treat, and cure any Midlandian who needed her. **As for Brushy...**

...Brushy became a unique kind of doctor.
"I'm a dentist!" he exclaimed.
As a dentist, Brushy made sure that every
smile in Midlandia stayed clean and sparkly.

From then on, the twins worked side by side. Fixit kept bodies healthy, and Brushy kept teeth healthy.

"May I borrow a tongue depressor, sis?" Brushy asked.

"Of course," Fixit replied. "We're a team."

"We're more than just a team," Brushy said. **"We're a family!"**

DISCUSSION QUESTIONS

Do you have any brothers or sisters?
How are you similar to your other family members?
How are you different?

Have you ever had trouble getting along with someone?
How did you try to solve your problems?

TWIN TROUBLE

Revised edition. First printing, January 2008.
Copyright 2020 © Lincoln Learning Solutions. All rights reserved.
294 Massachusetts Avenue
Rochester, PA 15074
Visit us on the web at http://www.lincolnlearningsolutions.org.
Midlandia® is a registered trademark of Lincoln Learning Solutions.

Edited by Ashley Mortimer
Character design by Evette Gabriel
Environmental design by Joshua Perry